ON BEING HUMAN

ON
BEING HUMAN

WOODROW WILSON
Ph.D., Litt.D., LL.D.
PRESIDENT OF THE UNITED STATES

HARPER & BROTHERS
NEW YORK AND LONDON
M · C · M · X · V · I

From the *Atlantic Monthly*
Copyright, 1897, by Houghton Mifflin & Co.

Printed in the United States of America
Published April, 1916

D–R

ON BEING HUMAN

ON BEING HUMAN

I

"THE rarest sort of a book," says
Mr. Bagehot, slyly, is "a book
to read"; and "the knack in style is
to write like a human being." It is
painfully evident, upon experiment,
that not many of the books which
come teeming from our presses every
year are meant to be read. They are
meant, it may be, to be pondered; it is
hoped, no doubt, they may instruct,
or inform, or startle, or arouse, or reform, or provoke, or amuse us; but
we read, if we have the true reader's

zest and palate, not to grow more knowing, but to be less pent up and bound within a little circle,—as those who take their pleasure, and not as those who laboriously seek instruction,—as a means of seeing and enjoying the world of men and affairs. We wish companionship and renewal of spirit, enrichment of thought and the full adventure of the mind; and we desire fair company, and a large world in which to find them.

No one who loves the masters who may be communed with and read but must see, therefore, and resent the error of making the text of any one of them a source to draw grammar from, forcing the parts of speech to stand out stark and cold from the warm text; or a store of samples whence to draw rhetorical instances, setting up figures of speech singly and without support of any neighbor phrase, to be stared at curiously and with intent to copy or dissect! Here is grammar done without deliberation: the phrases carry their meaning simply and by a sort of limpid reflection; the thought is a living thing, not an image ingeniously contrived and wrought. Pray leave the text whole: it has no meaning piecemeal; at any rate, not that best, wholesome meaning, as of a frank and genial friend who talks, not for himself or for his phrase, but for you. It is questionable morals to dismember a living frame to seek for its obscure fountains of life!

When you say that a book was

meant to be read, you mean, for one thing, of course, that it was not meant to be studied. You do not study a good story, or a haunting poem, or a battle song, or a love ballad, or any moving narrative, whether it be out of history or out of fiction—nor any argument, even, that moves vital in the field of action. You do not have to study these things; they reveal themselves, you do not stay to see how. They remain with you, and will not be forgotten or laid by. They cling like a personal experience, and become the mind's intimates. You devour a book meant to be read, not because you would fill yourself or have an anxious care to be nourished, but because it contains such stuff as it makes the mind hungry to look

upon. Neither do you read it to kill
time, but to lengthen time, rather,
adding to it its natural usury by
living the more abundantly while
it lasts, joining another's life and
thought to your own.

There are a few children in every
generation, as Mr. Bagehot reminds
us, who think the natural thing to
do with *any* book is to read it.
"There is an argument from design
in the subject," as he says; "if the
book was not meant for that purpose, for what purpose was it
meant?" These are the young eyes
to which books yield up a great
treasure, almost in spite of themselves, as if they had been pene-
trated by some swift, enlarging power of vision which only the young
know. It is these youngsters to

whom books give up the long ages of history, "the wonderful series going back to the times of old patriarchs with their flocks and herds"—I am quoting Mr. Bagehot again—"the keen-eyed Greek, the stately Roman, the watching Jew, the uncouth Goth, the horrid Hun, the settled picture of the unchanging East, the restless shifting of the rapid West, the rise of the cold and classical civilization, its fall, the rough impetuous Middle Ages, the vague warm picture of ourselves and home. When did we learn these? Not yesterday nor to-day, but long ago, in the first dawn of reason, in the original flow of fancy." Books will not yield to us so richly when we are older. The argument from design fails. We return to the staid authors we read long ago, and do not find in them the vital, speaking images that used to lie there upon the page. Our own fancy is gone, and the author never had any. We are driven in upon the books *meant* to be read.

These are books written by human beings, indeed, but with no general quality belonging to the kind—with a special tone and temper, rather, a spirit out of the common, touched with a light that shines clear out of some great source of light which not every man can uncover. We call this spirit human because it moves us, quickens a like life in ourselves, makes us glow with a sort of ardor of self-discovery. It touches the springs of fancy or of action within us, and makes our own life seem more quick and vital. We do not call every book

that moves us human. Some seem
written with knowledge of the black
art, set our base passions aflame, dis-
close motives at which we shudder—
the more because we feel their reality
and power; and we know that this
is of the devil, and not the fruitage
of any quality that distinguishes us
as men. We are distinguished as
men by the qualities that mark us
different from the beasts. When we
call a thing human we have a spirit-
ual ideal in mind. It may not be an
ideal of that which is perfect, but it
moves at least upon an upland level
where the air is sweet; it holds an
image of man erect and constant,
going abroad with undaunted steps,
looking with frank and open gaze
upon all the fortunes of his day, feeling ever and again—

[8]

ON BEING HUMAN

> "the joy
> Of elevated thoughts; a sense sublime
> Of something far more deeply interfused,
> Whose dwelling is the light of setting suns,
> And the round ocean and the living air,
> And the blue sky, and in the mind of man:
> A motion and a spirit, that impels
> All thinking things."

Say what we may of the errors and the degrading sins of our kind, we do not willingly make what is worst in us the distinguishing trait of what is human. When we declare, with Bagehot, that the author whom we love writes like a human being, we are not sneering at him; we do not say it with a leer. It is in token of admiration, rather. He makes us *like* our humankind. There is a noble passion in what he says, a wholesome humor that echoes genial comradeships; a certain reasonableness and moderation in what is thought and said; an air of the open day, in which things are seen whole and in their right colors, rather than of the close study or the academic class-room. We do not want our poetry from grammarians, nor our tales from philologists, nor our history from theorists. Their human nature is subtly transmuted into something less broad and catholic and of the general world. Neither do we want our political economy from tradesmen nor our statesmanship from mere politicians, but from those who see more and care for more than these men see or care for.

II

ONCE—it is a thought which troubles us—once it was a simple enough matter to be a human being, but now it is deeply difficult; because life was once simple, but is now complex, confused, multifarious. Haste, anxiety, preoccupation, the need to specialize and make machines of ourselves, have transformed the once simple world, and we are apprised that it will not be without effort that we shall keep the broad human traits which have so far made the earth habitable. We have seen our modern life accumulate, hot and

2

restless, in great cities—and we cannot say that the change is not natural: we see in it, on the contrary, the fulfilment of an inevitable law of change, which is no doubt a law of growth, and not of decay. And yet we look upon the portentous thing with a great distaste, and doubt with what altered passions we shall come out of it. The huge, rushing, aggregate life of a great city—the crushing crowds in the streets, where friends seldom meet and there are few greetings; the thunderous noise of trade and industry that speaks of nothing but gain and competition, and a consuming fever that checks the natural courses of the kindly blood; no leisure anywhere, no quiet, no restful ease, no wise repose—all this shocks us. It is inhumane. It does not seem human. How much more likely does it appear that we shall find men sane and human about a country fireside, upon the streets of quiet villages, where all are neighbors, where groups of friends gather easily, and a constant sympathy makes the very air seem native! Why should not the city seem infinitely *more* human than the hamlet? Why should not human traits the more abound where human beings teem millions strong?

Because the city curtails man of his wholeness, specializes him, quickens some powers, stunts others, gives him a sharp edge, and a temper like that of steel, makes him unfit for nothing so much as to sit still. Men have indeed written like human beings in the midst of great cities, but not often when they have shared the city's characteristic life, its struggle for place and for gain. There are not many places that belong to a city's life to which you can "invite your soul." Its haste, its preoccupations, its anxieties, its rushing noise as of men driven, its ringing cries, distract you. It offers no quiet for reflection; it permits no retirement to any who share its life. It is a place of little tasks, of narrowed functions, of aggregate and not of individual strength. The great machine dominates its little parts, and its Society is as much of a machine as its business.

"This tract which the river of Time
Now flows through with us, is the plain.
Gone is the calm of its earlier shore.
Border'd by cities, and hoarse

ON BEING HUMAN

With a thousand cries is its stream.
And we on its breasts, our minds
Are confused as the cries which we hear,
Changing and shot as the sights which we see.

   "And we say that repose has fled
Forever the course of the river of Time,
That cities will crowd to its edge
In a blacker, incessanter line;
That the din will be more on its banks,
Denser the trade on its stream,
Flatter the plain where it flows,
Fiercer the sun overhead,
That never will those on its breast
See an ennobling sight,
Drink of the feeling of quiet again.

   "But what was before us we know not,
And we know not what shall succeed.

   "Haply, the river of Time—
As it grows, as the towns on its **marge**
Fling their wavering lights
On a wider, statelier stream—

May acquire, if not the calm
Of its early mountainous shore,
Yet a solemn peace of its own.

 "And the width of the waters, the hush
Of the gray expanse where he floats,
Freshening its current and spotted with foam
As it draws to the Ocean, may strike
Peace to the soul of the man on its breast—
As the pale waste widens around him,
As the banks fade dimmer away,
As the stars come out, and the night-wind
Brings up the stream
Murmurs and scents of the infinite sea."

We cannot easily see the large
measure and abiding purpose of the
novel age in which we stand young
and confused. The view that shall
clear our minds and quicken us to
act as those who know their task and
its distant consummation will come
with better knowledge and completer

self-possession. It shall not be a night-wind, but an air that shall blow out of the widening east and with the coming of the light, that shall bring us, with the morning, "murmurs and scents of the infinite sea." Who can doubt that man has grown more and more human with each step of that slow process which has brought him knowledge, self-restraint, the arts of intercourse, and the revelations of real joy? Man has more and more lived with his fellow-men, and it is society that has humanized him—the development of society into an infinitely various school of discipline and ordered skill. He has been made more human by schooling, by growing more self-possessed—less violent, less tumultuous; holding himself in hand, and

moving always with a certain poise
of spirit; not forever clapping his
hand to the hilt of his sword, but
preferring, rather, to play with a
subtler skill upon the springs of
action. This is our conception of
the truly human man: a man in
whom there is a just balance of
faculties, a catholic sympathy—no
brawler, no fanatic, no pharisee; not
too credulous in hope, not too des-
perate in purpose; warm, but not
hasty; ardent, and full of definite
power, but not running about to be
pleased and deceived by every new
thing.

It is a genial image, of men we
love—an image of men warm and
true of heart, direct and unhesitat-
ing in courage, generous, magnani-
mous, faithful, steadfast, capable of

a deep devotion and self-forgetful-
ness. But the age changes, and with
it must change our ideals of human
quality. Not that we would give up
what we have loved: we would add
what a new life demands. In a new
age men must acquire a new capacity,
must be men upon a new scale, and
with added qualities. We shall need
a new Renaissance, ushered in by a
new "humanistic" movement, in
which we shall add to our present
minute, introspective study of ourselves, our jails, our slums, our nerve-
centers, our shifts to live, almost as
morbid as mediæval religion, a re-
discovery of the round world, and of
man's place in it, now that its face
has changed. We study the world,
but not yet with intent to school our
hearts and tastes, broaden our na-

tures, and know our fellow-men as comrades rather than as phenomena; with purpose, rather, to build up bodies of critical doctrine and provide ourselves with theses. That, surely, is not the truly humanizing way in which to take the air of the world. Man is much more than a "rational being," and lives more by sympathies and impressions than by conclusions. It darkens his eyes and dries up the wells of his humanity to be forever in search of doctrine. We need wholesome, experiencing natures, I dare affirm, much more than we need sound reasoning.

III

TAKE life in the large view, and we are most reasonable when we seek that which is most wholesome and tonic for our natures as a whole; and we know, when we put aside pedantry, that the great middle object in life—the object that lies between religion on the one hand, and food and clothing on the other, establishing our average levels of achievement—the excellent golden mean, is, not to be learned, but to be human beings in all the wide and genial meaning of the term. Does the age hinder? Do its mazy inter-

ests distract us when we would plan
our discipline, determine our duty,
clarify our ideals? It is the more
necessary that we should ask ourselves what it is that is demanded of
us, if we would fit our qualities to
meet the new tests. Let us remind
ourselves that to be human is, for
one thing, to speak and act with a
certain note of genuineness, a quality mixed of spontaneity and intel-
ligence. This is necessary for wholesome life in any age, but particularly
amidst confused affairs and shifting
standards. Genuineness is not mere
simplicity, for that may lack vitality,
and genuineness does not. We ex-
pect what we call genuine to have
pith and strength of fiber. Genuineness is a quality which we sometimes mean to include when we speak

of individuality. Individuality is lost the moment you submit to passing modes or fashions, the creations of an artificial society; and so is genuineness. No man is genuine who is forever trying to pattern his life after the lives of other people— unless, indeed, he be a genuine dolt. But individuality is by no means the same as genuineness; for individuality may be associated with the most extreme and even ridiculous eccentricity, while genuineness we conceive to be always wholesome, balanced, and touched with dignity. It is a quality that goes with good sense and self-respect. It is a sort of robust moral sanity, mixed of elements both moral and intellectual. It is found in natures too strong to be mere trimmers and conformers,

too well poised and thoughtful to
fling off into intemperate protest and
revolt. Laughter is genuine which
has in it neither the shrill, hysterical
note of mere excitement nor the hard,
metallic twang of the cynic's sneer—
which rings in the honest voice of
gracious good humor, which is inno-
cent and unsatirical. Speech is genuine which is without silliness, affectation, or pretense. That character
is genuine which seems built by nature rather than by convention,
which is stuff of independence and
of good courage. Nothing spurious,
bastard, begotten out of true wed-
lock of the mind; nothing adulter-
ated and seeming to be what it is
not; nothing unreal, can ever get
place among the nobility of things
genuine, natural, of pure stock and

unmistakable lineage. It is a prerogative of every truly human being to come out from the low estate of those who are merely gregarious and of the herd, and show his innate powers cultivated and yet unspoiled —sound, unmixed, free from imitation; showing that individualization without extravagance which is genuineness.

But how? By what means is this self-liberation to be effected—this emancipation from affectation and the bondage of being like other people? Is it open to us to choose to be genuine? I see nothing insuperable in the way, except for those who are hopelessly lacking in a sense of humor. It depends upon the range and scale of your observation whether you can strike the balance of genuineness or not. If you live in a small and petty world, you will be subject to its standards; but if you live in a large world, you will see that standards are innumerable—some old, some new, some made by the noble-minded and made to last, some made by the weak-minded and destined to perish, some lasting from age to age, some only from day to day—and that a choice must be made among them. It is then that your sense of humor will assist you. You are, you will perceive, upon a long journey, and it will seem to you ridiculous to change your life and discipline your instincts to conform to the usages of a single inn by the way. You will distinguish the essentials from the accidents, and deem the accidents something meant for your amusement. The strongest natures do not need to wait for these slow lessons of observation, to be got by conning life: their sheer vigor makes it impossible for them to conform to fashion or care for times and seasons. But the rest of us must cultivate knowledge of the world in the large, get our offing, reach a comparative point of view, before we can become with steady confidence our own masters and pilots. The art of being human begins with the practice of being genuine, and following standards of conduct which the world has tested. If your life is not various and you cannot know the best people, who set the standards of sincerity, your reading at least can be various, and you may look at your little circle through the best books, under the guidance of writers who have known life and loved the truth.

IV

AND then genuineness will bring
serenity—which I take to be another mark of the right development
of the true human being, certainly in
an age passionate and confused as
this in which we live. Of course serenity does not always go with genuineness. We must say of Dr. Johnson that he was genuine, and yet we
know that the stormy tyrant of the
Turk's Head Tavern was not serene.
Carlyle was genuine (though that is
not quite the *first* adjective we should
choose to describe him), but of serenity he allowed cooks and cocks

and every modern and every ancient sham to deprive him. Serenity is a product, no doubt, of two very different things, namely, vision and digestion. Not the eye only, but the courses of the blood must be clear, if we would find serenity. Our word "serene" contains a picture. Its image is of the calm evening when the stars are out and the still night comes on; when the dew is on the grass and the wind does not stir; when the day's work is over, and the evening meal, and thought falls clear in the quiet hour. It is the hour of reflection—and it is human to reflect. Who shall contrive to be human without this evening hour, which drives turmoil out, and gives the soul its seasons of self-recollection? Serenity is not a thing to beget inaction. It only checks excitement and uncalculating haste. It does not exclude ardor or the heat of battle: it keeps ardor from extravagance, prevents the battle from becoming a mere aimless mêlée. The great captains of the world have been men who were calm in the moment of crisis; who were calm, too, in the long planning which preceded crisis; who went into battle with a serenity infinitely ominous for those whom they attacked. We instinctively associate serenity with the highest types of power among men, seeing in it the poise of knowledge and calm vision, that supreme heat and mastery which is without splutter or noise of any kind. The art of power in this sort is no doubt learned in hours of reflection, by those who are not born with it. What rebuke of aimless excitement there is to be got out of a little reflection, when we have been inveighing against the corruption and decadence of our own days, if only we have provided ourselves with a little knowledge of the past wherewith to balance our thought! As bad times as these, or any we shall see, have been reformed, but not by protests. They have been made glorious instead of shameful by the men who kept their heads and struck with sure self-possession in the fight. No age will take hysterical reform. The world is very human, not a bit given to adopting virtues for the sake of those who merely bemoan its vices, and we are most effective when we are most calmly in possession of our senses.

So far is serenity from being a thing of slackness or inaction that it seems bred, rather, by an equable energy, a satisfying activity. It may be found in the midst of that alert interest in affairs which is, it may be, the distinguishing trait of developed manhood. You distinguish man from the brute by his intelligent curiosity, his play of mind beyond the narrow field of instinct, his perception of cause and effect in matters to him indifferent, his appreciation of motive and calculation of results. He is interested in the world about him, and even in the great universe of which it forms a part, not merely as a thing he would use, satisfy his wants and grow great by, but as a field to stretch his mind in, for love of journeyings and excursions in the

large realm of thought. Your full-
bred human being loves a run afield
with his understanding. With what
images does he not surround himself
and store his mind! With what fond-
ness does he con travelers' tales and
credit poets' fancies! With what
patience does he follow science and
pore upon old records, and with what
eagerness does he ask the news of the
day! No great part of what he
learns immediately touches his own
life or the course of his own affairs:
he is not pursuing a business, but
satisfying as he can an insatiable
mind. No doubt the highest form
of this noble curiosity is that which
leads us, without self-interest, to look
abroad upon all the field of man's
life at home and in society, seeking
more excellent forms of government,

more righteous ways of labor, more
elevating forms of art, and which
makes the greater among us states-
men, reformers, philanthropists, art-
ists, critics, men of letters. It is
certainly human to mind your neighbor's business as well as your own.
Gossips are only sociologists upon a
mean and petty scale. The art of
being human lifts to a better level
than that of gossip; it leaves mere
chatter behind, as too reminiscent of
a lower stage of existence, and is
compassed by those whose outlook
is wide enough to serve for guidance
and a choosing of ways.

V

LUCKILY we are not the first human beings. We have come into a great heritage of interesting things, collected and piled all about us by the curiosity of past generations. And so our interest is select-ive. Our education consists in learn-ing intelligent choice. Our energies do not clash or compete: each is free to take his own path to knowledge. Each has that choice, which is man's alone, of the life he shall live, and finds out first or last that the art in living is not only to be genuine and one's own master, but also to learn

mastery in perception and prefer-
ence. Your true woodsman needs
not to follow the dusty highway
through the forest nor search for any
path, but goes straight from glade to
glade as if upon an open way, having
some privy understanding with the
taller trees, some compass in his
senses. So there is a subtle craft in
finding ways for the mind, too. Keep
but your eyes alert and your ears
quick, as you move among men and
among books, and you shall find
yourself possessed at last of a new
sense, the sense of the pathfinder.
Have you never marked the eyes of
a man who has seen the world he has
lived in: the eyes of the sea-captain,
who has watched his life through the
changes of the heavens; the eyes of
the huntsman, nature's gossip and

familiar; the eyes of the man of affairs, accustomed to command in moments of exigency? You are at once aware that they are eyes which can see. There is something in them that you do not find in other eyes, and you have read the life of the man when you have divined what it is. Let the thing serve as a figure. So ought alert interest in the world of men and thought to serve each one of us that we shall have the quick perceiving vision, taking meanings at a glance, reading suggestions as if they were expositions. You shall not otherwise get full value of your humanity. What good shall it do you else that the long generations of men which have gone before you have filled the world with great store of everything that may make you

wise and your life various? Will you
not take usury of the past, if it may
be had for the taking? Here is the
world humanity has made: will you
take full citizenship in it, or will you
live in it as dull, as slow to receive,
as unenfranchised, as the idlers for
whom civilization has no uses, or the
deadened toilers, men or beasts,
whose labor shuts the door on choice?

That man seems to me a little less
than human who lives as if our life
in the world were but just begun,
thinking only of the things of sense,
recking nothing of the infinite throng-
ing and assemblage of affairs the
great stage over, or of the old wisdom
that has ruled the world. That is, if
he have the choice. Great masses of
our fellow-men are shut out from
choosing, by reason of absorbing toil,

and it is part of the enlightenment of
our age that our understandings are
being opened to the workingman's
need of a little leisure wherein to
look about him and clear his vision
of the dust of the workshop. We
know that there is a drudgery which
is inhuman, let it but encompass the
whole life, with only heavy sleep between task and task. We know that
those who are so bound can have no
freedom to be men, that their very
spirits are in bondage. It is part of
our philanthropy—it should be part
of our statesmanship—to ease the
burden as we can, and enfranchise
those who spend and are spent for
the sustenance of the race. But what
shall we say of those who are free
and yet choose littleness and bondage, or of those who, though they

might see the whole face of society, nevertheless choose to spend all a life's space poring upon some single vice or blemish? I would not for the world discredit any sort of philanthropy except the small and churlish sort which seeks to reform by nagging—the sort which exaggerates petty vices into great ones, and runs atilt against windmills, while everywhere colossal shams and abuses go unexposed, unrebuked. Is it because we are better at being common scolds than at being wise advisers that we prefer little reforms to big ones? Are we to allow the poor personal habits of other people to absorb and quite use up all our fine indignation? It will be a bad day for society when sentimentalists are encouraged to suggest all the measures that shall be taken for the betterment of the race. I, for one, sometimes sigh for a generation of "leading people" and of good people who shall see things steadily and see them whole; who shall show a handsome justness and a large sanity of view, an opportune tolerance for the details, that happen to be awry, in order that they may spend their energy, not without self-possession, in some generous mission which shall make right principles shine upon the people's life. They would bring with them an age of large moralities, a spacious time, a day of vision.

Knowledge has come into the world in vain if it is not to emancipate those who may have it from narrowness, censoriousness, fussiness, an intemperate zeal for petty things. It

would be a most pleasant, a truly
humane world, would we but open
our ears with a more generous wel-
come to the clear voices that ring in
those writings upon life and affairs
which mankind has chosen to keep.
Not many splenetic books, not many
intemperate, not many bigoted, have
kept men's confidence; and the mind
that is impatient, or intolerant, or
hoodwinked, or shut in to a petty
view shall have no part in carrying
men forward to a true humanity,
shall never stand as examples of the
true humankind. What is truly human has always upon it the broad
light of what is genial, fit to support
life, cordial, and of a catholic spirit of
helpfulness. Your true human being
has eyes and keeps his balance in the
world; deems nothing uninteresting

4 [43]

that comes from life; clarifies his
vision and gives health to his eyes by
using them upon things near and
things far. The brute beast has but
a single neighborhood, a single, narrow round of existence; the gain of
being human accrues in the choice of
change and variety and of experience far and wide, with all the world
for stage—a stage set and appointed
by this very art of choice—all future
generations for witnesses and audi-
ence. When you talk with a man
who has in his nature and acquire-
ments that freedom from constraint
which goes with the full franchise of
humanity, he turns easily from topic
to topic; does not fall silent or dull
when you leave some single field of
thought such as unwise men make a
prison of. The men who will not

be broken from a little set of subjects, who talk earnestly, hotly, with a sort of fierceness, of certain special schemes of conduct, and look coldly upon everything else, render you infinitely uneasy, as if there were in them a force abnormal and which rocked toward an upset of the mind; but from the man whose interest swings from thought to thought with the zest and poise and pleasure of the old traveler, eager for what is new, glad to look again upon what is old, you come away with faculties warmed and heartened—with the feeling of having been comrade for a little with a genuine human being. It is a large world and a round world, and men grow human by seeing all its play of force and folly.

VI

LET no one suppose that efficiency is lost by such breadth and catholicity of view. We deceive ourselves with instances, look at sharp crises in the world's affairs, and imagine that intense and narrow men have made history for us. Poise, balance, a nice and equable exercise of force, are not, it is true, the things the world ordinarily seeks for or most applauds in its heroes. It is apt to esteem that man most human who has his qualities in a certain exaggeration, whose courage is passionate, whose generosity is without deliberation, whose just action is without premeditation, whose spirit runs toward its favorite objects with an infectious and reckless ardor, whose wisdom is no child of slow prudence. We love Achilles more than Diomedes, and Ulysses not at all. But these are standards left over from a ruder state of society: we should have passed by this time the Homeric stage of mind—should have heroes suited to our age. Nay, we have erected different standards, and do make a different choice, when we see in any man fulfilment of our real ideals. Let a modern instance serve as test. Could any man hesitate to say that Abraham Lincoln was more human than William Lloyd Garrison? Does not every one know that it was the practical Free-Soilers who made emancipation possible,

and not the hot, impracticable Aboli-
tionists; that the country was infinitely more moved by Lincoln's tem-
perate sagacity than by any man's
enthusiasm, instinctively trusted the
man who saw the whole situation and
kept his balance, instinctively held
off from those who refused to see
more than one thing? We know how
serviceable the intense and headlong
agitator was in bringing to their feet
men fit for action; but we feel uneasy while he lives, and vouchsafe
him our full sympathy only when he
is dead. We know that the genial
forces of nature which work daily,
equably, and without violence are infinitely more serviceable, infinitely
more admirable, than the rude violence of the storm, however necessary
or excellent the purification it may

have wrought. Should we seek to name the most human man among those who led the nation to its struggle with slavery, and yet was no statesman, we should, of course, name Lowell. We know that his humor went further than any man's passion toward setting tolerant men atingle with the new impulses of the day. We naturally hold back from those who are intemperate and can never stop to smile, and are deeply reassured to see a twinkle in a reformer's eye. We are glad to see earnest men laugh. It breaks the strain. If it be wholesome laughter, it dispels all suspicion of spite, and is like the gleam of light upon running water, lifting sullen shadows, suggesting clear depths.

Surely it is this soundness of nature, this broad and genial quality, this full-blooded, full-orbed sanity of spirit, which gives the men we love that wide-eyed sympathy which gives hope and power to humanity, which gives range to every good quality and is so excellent a credential of genuine manhood. Let your life and your thought be narrow, and your sympathy will shrink to a like scale. It is a quality which follows the seeing mind afield, which waits on experience. It is not a mere sentiment. It goes not with pity so much as with a penetrative understanding of other men's lives and hopes and temptations. Ignorance of these things makes it worthless. Its best tutors are observation and experience, and these serve only those who keep clear eyes and a wide field of vision.

It is exercise and discipline upon such a scale, too, which strengthen, which for ordinary men come near to creating, that capacity to reason upon affairs and to plan for action which we always reckon upon finding in every man who has studied to perfect his native force. This new day in which we live cries a challenge to us. Steam and electricity have reduced nations to neighborhoods; have made travel pastime, and news a thing for everybody. Cheap printing has made knowledge a vulgar commodity. Our eyes look, almost without choice, upon the very world itself, and the word "human" is filled with a new meaning. Our ideals broaden to suit the wide day in which we live. We crave, not cloistered virtue—it is impossible any longer to keep to the cloister—but a robust spirit that shall take the air in the great world, know men in all their kinds, choose its way amid the bustle with all self-possession, with wise genuineness, in calmness, and yet with the quick eye of interest and the quick pulse of power. It is again a day for Shakespeare's spirit—a day more various, more ardent, more provoking to valor and every large design, even than "the spacious times of great Elizabeth," when all the world seemed new; and if we cannot find another bard, come out of a new Warwickshire, to hold once more the mirror up to nature, it will not be because the stage is not set for him. The time is such an one as he might rejoice to look upon; and if we would serve it as it should be served, we should seek to be human after his wide-eyed sort. The serenity of power; the naturalness that is nature's poise and mark of genuineness; the unsleeping interest in all affairs, all fancies, all things believed or done; the catholic understanding, tolerance, enjoyment, of all classes and conditions of men; the conceiving imagination, the planning purpose, the creating thought, the wholesome, laughing humor, the quiet insight, the universal coinage of the brain—are not these the marvelous gifts and qualities we mark in Shakespeare when we call him the greatest among men? And shall not these rounded and perfect powers serve us as our ideal of what it is to be a finished human being?

We live for our own age—an age

like Shakespeare's, when an old
world is passing away, a new world
coming in—an age of new specula-
tion and every new adventure of the
mind; a full stage, an intricate plot,
a universal play of passion, an out-
come no man can foresee. It is to
this world, this sweep of action, that
our understandings must be stretched
and fitted; it is in this age we
must show our human quality. We
must measure ourselves by the task,
accept the pace set for us, make shift
to know what we are about. How
free and liberal should be the scale
of our sympathy, how catholic our
understanding of the world in which
we live, how poised and masterful
our action in the midst of so great
affairs! We should school our ears to
know the voices that are genuine,

our thought to take the truth when it is spoken, our spirits to feel the zest of the day. It is within our choice to be with mean company or with great, to consort with the wise or with the foolish, now that the great world has spoken to us in the literature of all tongues and voices. The best selected human nature will tell in the making of the future, and the art of being human is the art of freedom and of force.

THE END